Parfait, NOT PARFAIT!

SCOTT ROTHMAN illustrated by **AVERY MONSEN**

Roaring Brook Press
New York

Parfait.

Not parfait.

Parfait.

Not parfait.

Shar-Pei.

Not Shar-Pei.

Toupee.

Shar-Pei toupee.

Parfait.

Not parfait.

Horseplay.

Wrong way!
Wrong way!

Shar-Pei poo-pay!

Parfait.

Not parfait.

Gourmet buffet.

SOUFFLÉ

COMTÉ

PURÉE

SORBET

Parfait.

Not parfait.

SPORK.

For Jen — S.R.
For Maisie — A.M.

Published by Roaring Brook Press
Roaring Brook Press is a division of
Holtzbrinck Publishing Holdings Limited Partnership
120 Broadway, New York, NY 10271 • mackids.com

Text copyright © 2022 by Scott Rothman
Illustrations copyright © 2022 by Avery Monsen
All rights reserved.

ISBN 978-1-250-26581-4
Library of Congress Control Number 2021047579

Our books may be purchased in bulk for
promotional, educational, or business use.
Please contact your local bookseller or
the Macmillan Corporate and
Premium Sales Department at
(800) 221-7945 ext. 5442 or by email at
MacmillanSpecialMarkets@macmillan.com.

First edition, 2022
Printed in China by RR Donnelley Asia Printing
Solutions Ltd., Dongguan City, Guangdong Province

10 9 8 7 6 5 4 3 2 1

ABOUT THIS BOOK The illustrations were created with a combination of acrylic paint on paper and digital paint on an iPad.
This book was edited by Connie Hsu and designed by Ashley Caswell with art direction by Jen Keenan and Neil Swaab.
The production was supervised by Allene Cassagnol, and the production editor was Jennifer Healey. The text was set in
KG Second Chances Solid, and the display types are WaveeWeekend, Brandon Grotesque Cond, and Vinyl.

Did you find . . . ?

blue jay • parquet • Norway • André • harp A • birthday • Sunday • Brontë • Hemingway
bird of prey • crochet • hair spray • Santa Fe • Pin the Tail on the Don-kay • beret • soufflé
Comté • purée • sorbet • sauté • fillet • spaghet-tay • ballet • bouquet • Hooray!